Foolproof

Foolproof

Diane Tullson

orca soundings

ORCA BOOK PUBLISHERS

Library and Archives Canada Cataloguing in Publication

Tullson, Diane, 1958–, author
Foolproof / Diane Tullson.
(Orca soundings)

Issued in print and electronic formats.
ISBN 978-1-4598-1034-1 (pbk.).—ISBN 978-1-4598-1036-5 (pdf).—
ISBN 978-1-4598-1037-2 (epub)

I. Title. II. Series: Orca soundings
PS8589.U6055F66 2015   jC813'.6   C2015-901710-6
C2015-901711-4

First published in the United States, 2015
Library of Congress Control Number: 2015935520

Summary: When Daniel falls for the hottest girl in school,
he ends up unwittingly running drugs across the border.

MIX
Paper from
responsible sources
FSC® C016245

*Orca Book Publishers is dedicated to preserving the environment and has
printed this book on Forest Stewardship Council® certified paper.*

Orca Book Publishers gratefully acknowledges the support for its publishing
programs provided by the following agencies: the Government of Canada through
the Canada Book Fund and the Canada Council for the Arts,
and the Province of British Columbia through the BC Arts Council
and the Book Publishing Tax Credit.

Cover image by iStock

ORCA BOOK PUBLISHERS
www.orcabook.com

Printed and bound in Canada.

18 17 16 15 • 4 3 2 1

For Steve, in memory

Chapter One

I leave work and do up my jacket, not so much because it's cool out but because I don't want my uniform to show. I don't need someone on the bus thinking it's hilarious to place a burger order with me. In the parking lot, a horn honks. It's Cyn Hawley in her white Honda Civic. She got an order at my drive-through window earlier. It's a nice Civic—flat-black hood, front spoiler. And Cyn Hawley is a nice-looking girl. She unrolls her window and leans out. "Want a ride?"

Cyn's hair is in a ponytail, and a few dark strands blow loose in the breeze. I look around to see if she's talking to me. She grins. "Daniel, right? Come on."

I walk over to the passenger side and open the door. "Thanks."

She moves her pack off the seat so I can get in. The interior is pristine. She says, "I went through your drive-through earlier."

"Large coffee with cream and two sugars." My face gets hot when I realize how lame I must seem to remember exactly what she ordered.

She laughs and reverses out of the stall. "Bio 12, right?"

In Bio, Cyn works with a group of girls at the next lab station. I nod. "Worst class ever." Then I add, "Not because of you." My face feels like it is bright red.

"Because of the nearly pervy Mr. Hetherington. That guy likes his latex gloves."

I laugh. "I haven't finished even one of his totally obscure lab experiments."

She merges onto Main, shifting smoothly through the gears. She's wearing tights that stretch smoothly over her thighs. I say, "I'm on the other side of the school, past the park. It's kind of far."

She waves her hand. She's wearing nail polish the color of amber sea glass. "I've got no place to be." She moves around a slow-moving truck, gearing down and touching the gas. The car responds.

"Whoa. This thing has some guts."

She glances at me. "You drive?"

"I have my license. No car though."

"Did you get the one with the extra ID? The one you can use at the border without a passport?"

I nod. Living right on the border, I think everyone in this town gets the enhanced license. "My sister told me to get it so I don't need a passport to go across the line. She lets me use her car sometimes, but I've got to put gas in it. Gas is so much cheaper across the line. With the enhanced license, you can just go."

"Yup. I always go across for gas." She gets a dreamy look on her face. "And Malabar."

"Huh?"

"You've never had a Malabar?"

I shake my head.

She says, "So much to learn. It's only the best chocolate in the world. Not easy to get though."

"My mom is making a soup for tonight that has chocolate in it. She's made it before. It sounds wrong, but it's really good."

"Like, for supper?"

"Yes. It's got black beans and peppers."

"And chocolate. Mmm, that sounds amazing."

"You should come."

The words were out before I could stop them. Why would Cyn want to eat with me and my family? I can barely look at her, in case she's rolling her eyes. I say, "Of course, you don't have to. I mean, it is short notice. And my family is nuts. My sister and her kid live with us. You probably have plans."

But she says, "I would love to."

The way she says it, it's like she really means it. I send a quick text to Mom, asking if I can bring someone. Her message back is just **xoxo**, her generic yes. I give Cyn directions to our street. We drive past the school, then Meridian Park. Police tape still dangles from a few trees. There was a shooting there last week—some minor gangster guy, not even that old. Normally, people from school use that parking lot because the few spots in front of the school are reserved for staff. Last week everyone had to park on the street.

We get to my building, and as we climb the stairs I think about the uniform I'm wearing. Maybe I can keep my jacket on. I open our door, and Livy launches herself off the couch, where she's been watching a kids' show. I scoop her up and she squeals, "Uncle Daniel!" She squashes her cheek against mine. I say to Cyn, "This is Livy, my sister's girl."

"Who's that?" Livy says, looking at Cyn.

Cyn is taking off her runners. She pauses. "I'm Cyn. I'm Daniel's friend."

Livy sings, "Cin, Cin, Cinderella."

Cyn laughs. She puts her runners by the stack of shoes at the front door. "It's Cynthia, actually, and I'm no princess." She looks around for a place to put her keys. I point to a key rack on the wall. There's a toy set of Livy's hanging on a hook. Cyn hangs her beside Livy's.

My jacket is still done up to my chin. "Uh, just give me five to change, okay?"

"Sure."

To Livy I say, "Maybe you could introduce Cyn to Gram."

Livy wriggles out of my arms and grabs Cyn's hand. She yells, "Gram, Uncle Daniel brought a girl home!"

From the kitchen I hear my mother say, "A girl?"

God. I hustle to my room and peel off my uniform. I sniff my armpits. I could use a shower, but there's no time. I grab a T-shirt I got at the thrift store and take off the price tag. Seven bucks, and it is brand new. I duck into the bathroom. Livy's tub toys are strewn all over the floor from her bath. I douse a towel and use it like a giant washcloth, hoping it will get most of the burger smell off me. I rake my damp hair with my fingers and then slather on deodorant. I put on the clean T-shirt and go back out to the kitchen.

My mother is at the stove, stirring the soup. Cyn is helping Livy set the table. My sister has arrived home—I noticed her keys on the rack as I went past and a stack of textbooks on the floor. She's leaning against the kitchen counter, taking in my hair and the clean T-shirt, a small smirk on her face. I ignore her and give my mother a hug. I say to Cyn, "You've met my mother? And this is my sister, Megan."

Cyn says, "Just now, yes." If she's aware of Megan's appraising stare, she doesn't show it.

My mother says, "Cyn was telling us she works at Dove's."

My sister says, "So you're both in the restaurant business."

I send Megan a *shut up* look and take the basket of bread my mother hands me.

Mom says, "Dove's is a nice restaurant, I've heard."

Megan says, "I know Dove. He was a year ahead of me at school."

Mom says, "He's so young to have his own restaurant."

"He used to sell dope in the parking lot," Megan adds.

"Megan!" Mom scolds.

Cyn blinks.

I say to Megan, "And you would know that he sold drugs how?"

Mom puts her hands on her hips. "Enough, both of you."

Cyn clears her throat. "I don't know Dove that well. I just hostess there. I don't really know him at all."

Mom says, "People can change. It sounds like Dove is doing well now."

"His parents probably bought him the business," Megan scoffs. "His parents bought him a car in eleventh grade. A nice car too. He acted like he deserved it."

I glance at Cyn. She's looking down at the floor. I say, "There's nothing wrong with parents buying a car for their kid."

Cyn says, "That car I drive is actually my brother's. He lost his license for too many tickets, so I'm driving it for a while."

I say to Megan, "If someone bought you a nice car, you'd think you deserved it too."

"Daniel, Megan, that's enough." Mom starts dishing out the soup. "Please, let's sit."

Livy climbs up onto her chair. "At that restaurant do you eat doves?"

Cyn takes the seat beside her. "People eat steak mostly. And this incredible sticky-toffee dessert."

"I want to go to Dove's," says Livy.

Megan puts a bowl of soup in front of Livy, stirring it so it will cool. I sit across from Cyn. She smiles at me. Cyn's eyes are the color of amber sea glass too. I feel my sister watching me. I drop my gaze to my bowl and concentrate on eating without getting food all over my clean shirt.

Chapter Two

The school cafeteria rumbles with the noon-hour rush. Tables are crammed with people and trays and disgorged lunch bags. Where I sit with Maxwell, someone has left a half-eaten carton of pineapple yogurt in the middle of the table. As I eat my sandwich, I watch a glob of yogurt slip down the side of the carton like a pale yellow sun setting into the scarred surface of the table. Across from me, Maxwell has stopped eating and is looking at me with his mouth open. Remnants of his lunch string his teeth. For a guy who spends an hour every morning on his hair, Maxwell is the world's most gross eater.

Finally, Maxwell finds his voice. He says, "That is crazy. I don't even believe that story."

I shrug. "It's true. She picked me up from work, and we spent the whole evening together."

His left eyebrow creeps upward. "Cyn Hawley."

"Yes, Maxwell. Cyn Hawley."

He cups his hands around imaginary breasts. "Cyn Hawley from Bio."

I sigh. "Could you act more astonished?"

He sits back. "Crazy."

The blob of yogurt slumps onto the table. "Don't overthink it, Maxwell. People win the lottery."

"Maybe so. But you haven't even been in the game."

I can see I haven't convinced him, but I don't have to. Cyn appears and straddles the bench beside him. She sits down and plops an apple core into the pile of lunch debris in the middle of the table. "Hey," she says to him, and then turns to me. "Does your mom always cook like that? Because that was the best dinner ever."

Maxwell's mouth drops open again.

Cyn says to me, "I'm cutting classes this afternoon. It's too nice to be in school. Want to go for a drive?"

I glance at Maxwell. He's looking at me with both eyebrows raised. Once or twice I have faked being sick to miss school, but then I missed the whole day.

I've never actually cut class and left school in the middle of the day.

Cyn puts on pink lip gloss. She does that thing girls do with their lips when they put on lip gloss—like they are kissing themselves. I guess I'm staring, because she smiles at me. "So?"

"Yes." What classes am I missing, and who cares? "Sure. I'm in."

"Well." Maxwell snickers. "Mr. Responsible cuts loose."

Cyn ignores him. "Let's go." As she gets up, the edge of her top lifts to show a sliver of smooth skin. If I take my eyes off her, I'm afraid this will all dissolve like a dream. I scramble up from the table and follow her out.

We head toward the Meridian Park lot. She says, "Do you have your license with you? I need some gas."

I pat my wallet. "Yes."

"And I want to check out some runners."

"Uh, I have to work at four."

"No wait times at the border. Half hour down. Half hour back. I'll drop you off at work." She nudges me in the side. "We'll have lots of time, Mr. Responsible." She says it with a smile, so I smile back.

The October sun feels warm, and we ride with the windows down. We drive past a speed trap, but Cyn doesn't take her foot off the gas. I say, "Wow, that was close."

She says, "I'm not speeding. Trust me, I do not speed in this car." She checks the rearview mirror and then grins. "Someone got caught though."

I look behind to see the lights flashing on the cop car.

She says, "Plus, I figured cops would be there—I've seen them in that spot. People drive fast on this highway. One time a car blew past me and by the time I got to the speed trap, his car was hooked to a tow truck and on its way to impound." She shudders. "Very bad day for that guy."

She plays great tunes, and we talk music, and it is so easy, like we do this all the time.

We cross the border and pull into a Discount gas bar. She says, "I've got to go inside and prepay. You want something? A Pepsi?"

"No, I'm good." But I should probably buy her a Pepsi. I try to remember how much cash I have on my debit card—a few bucks maybe. "I'll come in with you."

The gas is cheap, but Cyn wants a Malabar, whatever that is, and it takes forever. First the worker says they're out of Malabar. Then Cyn asks him to check in the back. So we have to move the car off the gas pump and park in the gas station's one stall, right under a sickly tree shedding its leaves, and go back in and wait. The guy finally emerges looking like he's been crawling under stacks of boxes to get the Malabar.

Back in the car, Cyn rips into the wrapper and snaps off a corner of the bar. "Here." She leans close and presses the chocolate onto my tongue. I feel the tip of her finger brush my mouth. "Don't bite it. Just let it melt."

I try to be amazed, but it tastes pretty ordinary. But what she does next amazes me. She kisses me. Her lips take mine, gently at first, then her tongue finds every nerve ending in my body. I am almost out of breath when she releases me. "Mmm," she says. "Malabar is even better this way."

I try to stop blinking.

She says, "It's always worth waiting for the Malabar."

I sit there, stunned, thinking about her kissing me, as Cyn drives to a block of big-box stores. I follow her into the

Marshall's. In the shoe department, Cyn's a shark. She moves past rows of shiny heels straight to the runners. She scans the display and selects her style. She pulls the box, size seven, and takes it to a bench. She tries them on, jogging in place, jumping lightly, then goes to the mirror. She turns one foot to the side, checks it out, nods and says, "These will do." The whole shoe-shopping process takes about ninety seconds.

"That's it?" I say. "You don't want to try them in another color even?"

She looks at the shoes. "What's wrong with this color?"

"Nothing. It's just that when I shop with my sister, she has to try on every-thing in the store."

Cyn places the runners in their box. Her sock has a small hole in the toe. Her toenail looks like a pink pearl. "I always buy this kind of runners. I know what I like."

I go to a shelf of high-heeled sandals my sister would go nuts over. I select a pair with a slender ankle strap studded with crystals. I mimic my sister's reaction. "Oh my god, these are so cute!"

She laughs. "They are—not that I'd ever wear them."

I find her size and pass her the box. She looks at me. "You want me to try these on? Do you have some kind of weird foot thing?"

"Maybe." Maybe I have a weird thing for all of her. "Try them."

She says, "I actually hate shopping." With an exaggerated sigh she peels off her socks and slips her feet into the sandals. I kneel down to do up the straps for her. I let my thumbs linger a moment, and I feel a tiny pulse throbbing on the top of her left foot. She examines the shoes in the mirror. "These are definitely cute shoes." She slips the straps off and steps out of the sandals, tipping them back into their box. "But I don't wear shoes I can't run in."

I follow her to the checkout. "What about for work?"

"I wear flats. I'd wear runners if I could get away with it."

"Or to go out?"

She stops and turns to look at me. "Like on a date?"

My throat wants to stick together. "Yes, like a date. I'm not asking you out. I mean, I'd like to ask you, but it's probably too soon. I mean, you wouldn't want to go out. With me. I mean, if we were going out maybe you'd want to, but we're not going out. Are we?"

I sound like an absolute idiot. But she kisses me. It's a jolt of a kiss, quick and perfect, like a burst of match flame on my lips. I'm sure my eyes bug out. She says, "You should ask me out. I'd say yes."

Chapter Three

Today I had Bio, a course I could grow to like because I can watch Cyn all class. During class she smiled at me a couple of times but didn't come over to talk. Maybe she doesn't want to be seen with me at school.

But tonight, I'm in a dead sleep and my phone wakes me up. I try to blink the sleep from my vision and reach for the phone. It's a text from Cyn.

Meet me at Meridian Park at one.

I text back, **As in tonight?**

Yes.

The house is quiet. I pull on some jeans and a hoodie and close the door softly behind me. I put my shoes on outside. The night air feels cold. I jam my hands in my pockets and walk fast to keep warm.

The lot at Meridian Park is empty. I stand in a circle of light.

She's not there. Wind creaks in the trees. I check the time—1:00 AM. Where is she? I hear a car and step back into the shadows, imagining a guy with a chainsaw. But it's her.

She parks, jumps out of the car and gives me a hug. "I hope it's not too late for you."

I lie. "I was just doing homework."

She takes my hand and pulls me through the darkness to sit on a bench a short distance from the parking lot. A light over the bench makes a yellow island in the night. There's enough light that I can see her, but it feels private. Cyn is wearing the same clothes she had on at school—jeans and a little T-shirt. I take off my hoodie and wrap it around her. I'm not sure it's the right thing to do, but I put my arm around her too. She smiles and snuggles in close to me. She says, "I couldn't wait a whole night to see you."

With what she is saying, and how she presses herself against me, the cold night air is gone, and all I feel is heat. I can't trust my voice, so I just nod. She pulls me closer. I shift a bit so she maybe won't feel what she's doing to me. She reaches up and runs her fingers against my lips. Her touch courses through me. I kiss her before I can think about it, before I can doubt that she wants to kiss me. And she kisses me back.

Her lips are soft and firm at the same time. She tastes like honey and salt. When we finally stop, she says, "I've been thinking about doing that since the first time I kissed you."

"Me too."

I don't know how long we are on the bench, but it's like no amount of time is enough. She pulls away first. She says, "You probably need to get home."

If anyone knew I was out this late with school tomorrow, I'd hear about it. But no one knows. I wonder how she gets away with being out so late. I say, "No, I'm fine." But the night feels suddenly cold, and I shiver.

She laughs. "Come on. I have something for you."

We walk to the car. She reaches into the backseat and pulls out a shopping bag. It's from the same store where she bought her runners.

"You went shopping again? I thought you didn't like shopping."

"I like shopping for you."

I must look like I'm stunned, because she says, "It's okay, Daniel. Look in the bag."

It's a jacket—a nice jacket, the kind you wear on a date.

"Wow." It's all I can think of to say. It looks expensive.

"Put it on."

The jacket is lined with satin that slides over my arms. The sleeves fall to exactly the right length on my wrists.

"It's perfect on you."

I find my voice. "You shouldn't spend your money on me."

"It was a deal. Plus I've been making great tips at work," she says. "I tried to buy a dress, but they didn't have my size. They're bringing one in from another store." She strokes the front of the jacket with her hands. "You look drop-dead gorgeous in it, Daniel."

I feel my face flush with her compliment. "It's way too much." I go to take off the jacket.

"You tell yourself whatever you like." She pulls the jacket back onto my shoulders and hands me the bag. "But I'm not taking it back. And anyway, you gave me your hoodie, so it's fair."

I didn't actually give her my hoodie, but if she wants it that makes me really happy.

She drops me at home, and I creep to my bedroom. Using just the light from my phone, I check out how I look in the jacket. It is a great jacket. It makes me look different. It makes me look good, almost. The price tag, though, makes my heart stop. Even at the sale price, I have never, ever bought something this expensive. I don't even want to think about my mother's reaction when she sees it. And my sister's. There is no way I'm going to tell them Cyn bought it for me.

I carefully take off the cardboard part of the price tag, leaving the plastic string that attaches to the jacket. Then I find the price tag from the T-shirt I got at the thrift store. The tag is stamped *New*. At seven bucks, the T-shirt was a good price. It is unbelievable that the thrift store would price such a nice jacket that low. But I have to hope it's believable enough for my mother and sister. I thread the thrift-store tag onto the jacket and hang it in my closet. The shopping bag I roll up into a ball and jam in the bottom of my pack. I'll get rid of it at school tomorrow.

School. I yawn. I am going to be so tired. But then I think about seeing Cyn, about how I will put my arm around her in the hall, how I'll kiss her and she'll kiss me, how everyone will know we're a couple. When you have a girl like Cyn, everything feels possible.

Chapter Four

I don't see Cyn before classes start. I hang out near her locker, but she doesn't show. I check my phone about a hundred times in case she texts, but there is nothing from her. When she's not at Bio, I drag myself to the lab station I share with Maxwell. He gives me a shove and says, "Don't be all needy, my friend."

The girls at the next lab station laugh. Is it that obvious? It's just that with Cyn, I don't know if it is real, what we have. I want to think it is real. I just need to see her again. To hold her. To know.

And then she is there, walking into the classroom. She tosses a late slip on the teacher's desk and slings her book bag down at the lab station with the girls. She's wearing my hoodie.

Maxwell flips his book open to the instructions for the experiment and starts to read. "What?" he says, rubbing his chin. "We're supposed to do what? With what?"

Cyn's hair is pulled back. Tiny strands of hair curl at the nape of her neck.

One of the girls, Mila, says, "Could there be more cops in the school today?"

Cyn's hands pause on her textbook, but she doesn't look up.

Another girl says, "I know! It's like they're interrogating us."

Mila says, "It's like they think we're *all* criminals."

Cyn closes her book and slides it down the table. She moves to where Maxwell and I still haven't started the experiment. "Okay if I join you guys?"

One of the girls mutters something. Mila says, "Whatever."

Cyn smells like the outdoors, like the morning air has followed her in. I feel my face grow warm. Maxwell looks at me and rolls his eyes. When I don't say anything, he turns to Cyn and says, "You can absolutely work with us. But full disclosure—we suck at Bio."

The girls seem to watch us, their heads together, talking softly. I move closer to Cyn. I don't know why, but I feel like I need to protect her. Cyn focuses on setting up the experiment. She actually knows what she's doing.

Maxwell says, "Oh! That's what that gizmo is for."

She laughs. "It's called a pipette." She points to the diagram in Maxwell's textbook. "You just have to set up the experiment exactly like in the book. Then it should work." She watches as Maxwell assembles the equipment. "That's perfect," she says.

Maxwell smiles. "Thanks."

"Just be careful with the iodine," she says. "It will stain your clothes."

Maxwell works through the steps of the experiment. I don't have to do anything but watch Cyn, which is fine with me. I like how she moves so sure and confident, how when she makes notes her handwriting slants backward, as if the letters are caught in the wind.

The girls at the other station are still talking about the cops.

I look at Maxwell. "So what's with the cops?"

He nods. "Because of the shooting at Meridian Park last week. They're interviewing people in case anyone saw something."

I say, "If someone saw something, they would have already reported it."

Maxwell says, "You'd think so, especially when people are getting shot right in our parking lot. I'm glad the cops are all over this."

One of the girls says, "So what if a drug dealer gets shot? It's one less drug dealer."

Maxwell says, "It doesn't sound like he was a big player. Poor bastard might have owed the wrong guy money." He calls over to the girls, "You want the cops just to let them shoot each other in our parking lot? What if one of us gets caught in the crossfire?"

Mila says, "Maxwell is right." She smiles at him. Maxwell stands up tall and puffs out his chest. He looks at me as if to say, *Can you believe this?* Mila is pretty, which makes it all the more amazing that she knows his name.

I feel Cyn's hand on my waist. Her touch is light and so brief that I'm not sure she meant to touch me. But then her fingers slip under my shirt and trace the top of my jeans. I glance at Maxwell, but he's busy watching Mila's butt as she bends over the work station. The rest of the classroom blurs as Cyn tugs my waistband. She says, "Walk me to my next class, okay?"

The bell rings and Maxwell slams his notebook closed. "That experiment was so easy!" I realize I haven't made a single note, and I don't even care. I grab my stuff and follow Cyn out of the classroom.

The hallway is packed and I almost have to run to keep up. A few people give me dirty looks as I shoulder past them. Where the hallways intersect, a couple of school liaison cops stand like big blue islands in the throng. Their arms are crossed, and they are scanning the crowd. One of them follows Cyn with his eyes. I don't know why, but I feel my face flush red. Cyn notices the cop too and ducks her head. The cop curls his finger at me, motioning me to come over. Cyn blows me a small sideways kiss and then disappears in the crowd.

The cop introduces himself as Constable Nagle, gives me his card and pulls out a tablet. He asks my name, what grade I'm in. I'm thinking about the cop watching Cyn, and how her fingers touched her lips as she blew the kiss. The cop tap-taps. Do I live near the school? Do I drive? Where do I park? I think about Cyn's fingers on my belly. The cop is just looking at me. Did he ask me something else? He seems to be waiting for me to answer.

"Huh?"

The cop sighs. "I said, when was the last time you were in Meridian Park?"

I think about last night, with Cyn, on the bench in Meridian Park. I think about the lamplight hanging in the trees and how the cold raised little bumps on Cyn's ski, and how warm she was when she held me. Just now, in the hallway, was she blowing me a kiss? Or was she shushing me? The cop raises his eyebrows. "Well?"

Why wouldn't Cyn want me to say anything to the cop? She and I were there last night, but the shooting was last week. We didn't see anything. We weren't doing anything wrong. But I don't really want to explain to the cop what we were doing there at one in the morning. I say, "Meridian Park? I can't remember the last time I was there."

Chapter Five

Two days later Cyn is standing at my locker, chewing on her thumbnail. As I approach, she smiles and throws her arms around me. She kisses me on the cheek. "How would you like to drive the Honda?"

"At lunch?"

She shakes her head. "Right now. It needs gas."

"Now? I've got a class. How about we go together at lunch?" I open my locker and reach for my textbook.

She puts her hand on mine. "No, it's got to be right now. My brother is picking it up, and he'll lose his mind if I haven't filled the tank. I'd go, but I've already skipped this week."

Has she forgotten that I've skipped too?

She says, "And I've been late. Twice." She presses the keys into my hands. "There's forty bucks in the console. Go to the same place. Park it at Meridian when you get back. My brother will get it there."

I'm just about to ask where to leave the keys when she says, "He's got keys."

The bell rings and she starts to walk away. I say, "Why don't you just give your brother the cash?"

She turns and runs back. She cradles my face with her hands and kisses me, full on, navigating the entire surface of my tongue. When she finally pulls back, I have to gasp for a breath. She says, "Because I really want a Malabar." She taps the end of my nose. "Remember the Malabar." Then the hallway is empty and classroom doors are closing, and I'll be late to class now anyway. I toss the keys in my hand. So I guess I'll go for a drive.

I keep the speedometer at ten over and stay with the flow of traffic, fast enough to learn what the car can do but not so fast that I attract attention. I downshift into the corners just for the feeling of the car uncoiling. I would so like to own this car. The border guard asks who owns the car, and for a second I sweat because I don't know Cyn's brother's name. I don't remember if we got asked this when Cyn and I crossed. I'm pretty sure we didn't. But when I give him the only name I know,

"Hawley," the guard waves me through. That was easy. I crank the sound system and imagine that I do own this car.

At the gas station the same worker is on, and he gives me the same hard time about not having any Malabar and then about not waiting on the pump while he takes for-fricking-ever getting the Malabar. And when he finally comes out with the Malabar, his shirt is covered in the same crud, like he's had to crawl through a warehouse again to get it. By the time I pay, I have just enough time to get back for second class. I pull into a spot at Meridian Park.

Cyn's brother. Who is this guy anyway? I reach over to the glove box and pull out the plastic pouch with the vehicle registration. He probably lives in a great condo with a great girlfriend and a great dog. Wait a minute. How is he going to get the car if he lost his license?

I slip the registration papers out of the pouch.

Her brother doesn't own the car. The owner is Cynthia Hawley.

Chapter Six

At supper, Megan looks jubilant, like she has news that no one else has. She can hardly wait until we're all seated before announcing, "Police were at Dove's asking about the gang shootings."

I say, "Police have been everywhere in this town. They were at the school interviewing us. Anyway, how do you know about police being at Dove's?"

"One of my clients at the salon works there. She told me."

"Dove's." Mom looks at me, her forehead creased with concern. "That's where your new friend works."

Before I can reply, Megan says, "Well, that's the thing. My friend doesn't know Cyn. She says she's never heard of her. Isn't that weird?"

Yes, that is weird. Very weird. Suddenly, I'm not hungry. I say, "Maybe they work different shifts." Or maybe she uses a different name. Or maybe she doesn't even work there. How would I know? I slip my phone out of my pocket and check the screen. Cyn still hasn't answered my texts.

Beside me, Livy says, "Who are you texting?"

"No one." I put the phone away before my mother can tell me to.

Megan notices me checking my phone too. She says, "You remember you're staying home with Livy tonight, right?"

Livy squeals with delight, "Uncle Daniel!" and thumps her hands on the table.

I say, "Like I do every Wednesday, yes, pro bono, and like I have since she was a baby because you're at class and Mom has choir." I gather Livy into a squirming heap and plunk her onto my lap. "And we're going to read *two* stories at bedtime."

Livy holds up three fingers. "Three!"

"You better get ready then."

Mom says to Livy, "Come on. Let's get you ready for bed before I go."

Livy scrambles down from my lap. When they are out of the room, I say to Megan, "Why did you have to ask me that? When have I ever not watched Livy when you've asked me? When have I ever let you down?"

Megan smirks. "Well, now that you have a girlfriend…"

I interrupt her. "Cyn and I are friends, okay? She's not my girlfriend. I mean, I've turned down shifts at work to stay home with Livy, and I don't care that I'm not getting paid. I do it because it's Livy. I will always be here to take care of Livy. Always."

Megan holds up her hands. "Okay, okay. I'm sorry."

I say, "Just don't act like you know Cyn or anything about her, okay? Because you don't."

Neither do I, apparently.

Later, when Mom and Megan have left and Livy is finally asleep, I hear from Cyn. She texts, **Can I come over?**

She must be parked outside, because I've no sooner replied than she's at the door. She glances around at the empty house, at the key rack with no keys

hanging on it, and says, "It's just us?"
She wraps her arms around my waist.

I push her away. "You didn't answer
my texts."

She takes my hands and sets them on
her hips. "My phone died." She nibbles
my ear. "Sorry."

Her lips feel soft and warm. I say,
"The Honda. Whose car is it, Cyn?"

"We've got the place to ourselves
and you want to talk about my car?" She
kisses me lightly along my cheek, then on
my lips. She tastes like peppermint gum.

"They asked at the border. Why did
you say it was your brother's?"

She moves my hands higher. "So
you wouldn't get all weird about me
having a car and you not having a car.
Like you are now." She presses herself
against my hands.

Gently, I push her away. "Tell me,
Cyn. Is it your car?"

"You'll just hate me if I tell you."

"I doubt that. Just don't lie to me."

Her shoulders slump. "What do you want me to say? That my parents bought it for me? That they buy me stuff to make themselves feel better because they're never around? That all I have to do is ask and they'll hand over whatever I want?" A tear slips down her cheek. "I don't even have a brother, Daniel. I wish I did. I wish I had someone who understood me and loved me just for breathing."

"Cyn…"

She continues, "I wish I had a brother who could buy me a car. But I had a boyfriend. He wasn't very nice, but he bought me stuff I could never have otherwise. He had so much, it was nothing to him. But it was everything to me."

I pull her close against my chest. "I'm sorry, okay?"

She sniffles. "Don't be jealous, okay? I'm not proud of being with him. And I don't care if you can't buy me stuff."

Until that minute it hadn't occurred to me that I am supposed to buy her stuff. None of Megan's boyfriends bought her anything. But then, they were all losers—they couldn't even buy condoms. Cyn bought me the jacket, so maybe I am supposed to get her presents. I say, "You're done with the guy, right?"

She mock-slaps my chest. "Yes, you dumbass. I'm with you."

"Well, it *is* a nice car."

She laughs a little.

I kiss the top of her head. "You can tell me what's going on with you. I live with women—I'm used to listening."

She steps back and pulls off her hoodie. "Ask me anything."

And everything I want to ask, everything I want to know, vanishes as she folds herself against me. I slide my hands over her thin T-shirt, tracing the even bumps of her spine. She winces. I yank my hands away. "Did I hurt you?" Just under the sleeve of her shirt, it looks like she has a big bruise. "What happened?"

She barely makes eye contact. "It's nothing. I just bumped myself." She reaches for my hand. "Come on. Let's watch TV. Or something." She grins.

We do watch TV, or something, and afterward I must have fallen asleep, because Cyn is shaking me awake, her keys in her hand.

"Cyn, is everything okay?"

"I just have to go, okay? I don't want to be here when Megan gets home. She won't be happy if I'm here while you're watching Livy."

In Livy and Megan's room, I hear Livy cry out.

"Oh no," I moan. "She must be having a dream."

Cyn puts her fingers to my lips. "I'll check on her."

I stand at the doorway while Cyn pads over to where Livy is thrashing in her sleep. Cyn puts her hand on Livy's back. "It's okay, sweetie. It's just a dream."

Livy sits up. "It was a monster. I couldn't run."

Cyn says, "I get those dreams too."

Livy stares at Cyn, as if she's trying to focus. "What are you doing here?"

Cyn smooths Livy's hair. "I was just hanging out with your uncle Daniel." She turns Livy's pillow over and plumps it up. "Your mom will be home soon."

Livy settles back on her pillow. "Mmm, that feels nice." She curls up on her side as Cyn straightens the blankets and tucks one of Livy's stuffies under her arm. Livy's voice already sounds half asleep when she says, "Uncle Daniel likes you."

Cyn looks over her shoulder at me and smiles. "I like him too."

Cyn stands watching Livy for a moment or two, and then she creeps out of the room, closing the door.

"Wow," I say. "You're like the kid whisperer. She never settles so quickly for me."

Cyn smiles. "But now I've really got to go."

Standing in the hall, wearing just my jeans, I'm suddenly self-conscious. I fold my arms across my chest, wishing I had a shirt. "Is everything okay with us? I'm sorry I fell asleep."

"You are such a nice guy, Daniel." She strokes the side of my face. "You make me feel like I am worth something." She kisses me softly, barely parting her lips.

When Cyn leaves, I peek in at Livy. She is still curled up asleep, her hair fanning the pillow, one arm still holding the stuffie that Cyn gave her.

Chapter Seven

At Bio, Cyn is a no-show. I have to redo the experiment from the last class because I didn't make any notes. Maxwell has already handed in the assignment. But does he help me? No. He abandons me to figure out the experiment on my own while he chats up Mila and the girls at the next lab station.

Then, at lunch, he's full of stories. He says, "That Dove guy Cyn works for?" He crams a sandwich into his mouth. "They went out. Apparently, he used to pick her up from school in a big-ass SUV."

Dove was the boyfriend? I feel my face get hot. "Maybe he was giving her a ride to work."

Maxwell shrugs. "I'm just telling you what I heard."

"From Mila and the girls in Bio?"

"Yes. They live in the same neighborhood. Mila and Cyn used to be best friends. Their parents are in Hawaii together as we speak. So I guess Mila would know if Cyn went out with Dove."

"It's also possible that Mila just thinks she knows what she's talking about."

Maxwell gives me a long look. "I like Mila."

"I'm sorry." I am. "But I don't know why you're talking about me with Mila."

He holds up his hands. "Whoa, it's not like we were discussing you. All Mila said was that she's glad Cyn is going out with a solid guy now. It sounds like Dove creeps her out."

I've never met the guy and he's starting to creep me out too.

I'm leaving school when I get a text from Cyn. She's waiting at her car in Meridian Park. By the time I get there, hers is the only car in the lot. She sees me and gets out and runs to meet me. She buries her face in my neck. I say, "Where were you today? Did you go to any of your classes?"

She shrugs. "I was there for part of the day. I had a dentist appointment."

"We could have met up."

"And walked around in the halls, holding hands?"

The way she says it, it sounds like maybe that's not the most exciting thing she's ever done. I say, "Well, I'd like that. We'd be like a normal couple."

"I'm not exactly normal, Daniel."

I think about the time we met here in the middle of the night. I remember last night. I kiss the top of her head. "You are extraordinary."

I feel her sigh.

"I'd settle for ordinary."

What Maxwell said at lunch about her dating Dove comes back to me. Dove must be at least four years older than her, already graduated, with his own business. I say, "So am I your ticket to ordinary?"

"I want to be a normal couple, Daniel, more than anything. I want to hang out and watch movies and, yes, I want to walk around the school holding hands."

"Would you go to the totally lame and ordinary dance with me next week?"

She grins. "Yes. And I'll even wear shoes with heels." She opens the passenger door and reaches behind the seat. She pulls out a bag. "Don't worry. This time I bought stuff for me."

I say, "You went across again today? For someone who hates shopping, you sure go a lot."

"My dress came in. And I bought those sandals you liked." She tugs the shoes out to show me. "So now I can go to the dance."

I hug her. "You could wear a garbage bag and still be the most beautiful girl there."

She slips her hands under my shirt. Her hands are cold, and I gasp. She laughs. "You are kind of extraordinary yourself." She's making me crazy with her touch. She says, "Anyone at your house?"

I groan. "Everyone is at my house. What about yours?"

She shudders. "I wish we could just go away." She tips her face to look at me. "Right now. Tonight. The two of us. We could get a tiny suite in the city."

I stroke her neck. "We'd both have to work two jobs to afford even a closet in the city."

"I would."

"And we'd have to take Livy."

She smiles. "I would."

By the time she takes me home, it's getting dark. She pulls up in front of the house. "Come on up," I say.

She shakes her head. "I'd love to, but I've got a ton of homework from missing class. Say hi to Livy for me."

She kisses me, and it's like I've always known the curve of her lips, the taste of her, the way her breath catches when I touch her.

I get out of the car and manage to drop my book bag. Then, as I grab my bag, my house keys drop out of the pocket and onto the ground. "Just a sec," I say. I have to reach under the car for the keys. When I stand up, she's looking at her phone, a small crease in her forehead. I say, "See you at school tomorrow, right?"

She looks at me and her face softens into a smile. "Ordinary, normal school."

She drives off, and I head into the house. As I'm hanging up my jacket, I notice something stuck to the sleeve. It is a strip of gray duct tape.

"Weird," I say to myself. "Where did that come from?"

It had to have come from the bottom of Cyn's car.

Chapter Eight

Something had been taped to the bottom of the car. Cyn has had that car across the border a half dozen times. You hear about people shopping across the line having stuff taped to their cars. They drive the stuff through the border, and the drug dealer follows them home. Or their car gets flagged for a border inspection and the stuff is found, and the fool gets charged with possession.

On the phone, Maxwell is unconcerned. I can hear the sound of a keyboard clicking—he's playing a game while he talks to me. He says, "You're the one who tells me not to overthink things, Daniel. I don't know anything about cars, but it's possible the tape was holding a broken tailpipe or something."

"Megan says Dove used to sell drugs. She says the cops were at his restaurant. Maybe he still deals."

More clicking. "And you really think Cyn is involved?"

"It's possible, Maxwell. Don't make it sound like I'm an idiot for thinking it."

He sighs. "You should just ask her."

"Ask her if she's running drugs across the border? For her drug-dealing boss and/or ex?" I sift through a pile of papers on my desk until I find the card

Constable Nagle gave me. I turn the card over and throw it face down on the pile.

Maxwell says, "You've covered more with Cyn than you have in your entire life. It's quite possible you'll never get this far again."

"Gee, thanks."

"Cyn is gorgeous. And she's smart. I got an A on the Bio lab—I want her to be our lab partner forever. And she likes you. So what is your problem? Anyway," Maxwell continues, "it's not like you've done anything wrong."

"Right." I hang up. I'm not so sure about that.

I text Cyn. **We have to talk**.

An hour later she picks me up. She puts her finger over my lips. "We'll go for a walk, okay?" So we go to Meridian Park. At the bench, she puts her arms around me. "This is our spot now." She brushes my lips with hers. "Where we first kissed."

"The first time we kissed we were at the gas bar."

"Details, details." Her tongue flicks my upper lip. "Kiss me now."

I want to kiss her. Every single part of me wants her. I have to make myself push her away. "Cyn, I'm probably crazy, but are you doing anything for Dove?"

Her eyes widen ever so slightly. "What do you mean, *doing anything*? He's my boss, Daniel. I work for him."

"I know. But are you *just* working? Like, just in the restaurant?"

She drops her arms. "What exactly are you asking?"

The night air feels suddenly cold without her arms around me. I say, "I know it sounds nuts. I'm sorry. It's just that Mila said you and Dove went out, and I just wonder if you're, you know, done with him."

"Oh, that." She laughs. "He thought I was older. I thought he was nicer."

She loops her arm in mine. "You had me scared, Daniel. I thought you were going to break up with me."

I wipe my hands on my pants. "Was he the boyfriend who bought you the car?"

She drops her arms to her sides and huffs. "You said I could tell you what's going on with me, and then you just throw it back at me."

"Don't do this, Cyn."

"Do what?"

"Don't make this about something else. I'm here with you because I want to be."

She puts her head against my shoulder. "I'm so glad you're here."

"I just have to know." I turn so we're facing each other. "Cyn, there was some tape on the bottom of your car."

She tilts her head. "Tape?"

I say, "Earlier, when you drove me home, I dropped my keys when I got out of the car. I had to reach under your car to get them, and a piece of tape stuck to me. And I was thinking about the guy at the Discount gas bar, how his shirt is always dirty, like he's been lying on the ground where a tree has been dropping its leaves. Like where you always park. Like where I parked when I went there for you."

She doesn't look at me when she speaks. "Don't think too hard, Daniel."

I shake my head. "No. Tell me. What are you doing, Cyn? What am *I* doing?"

Now she turns. Her eyes seem icy. "If I tell you, then you'll never be able to say that you didn't know."

It's cold, but sweat runs down my back. "That's the thing. I know something is happening. I know you're involved, and probably so am I, and it is not good."

"So you know. Great. Can we leave it at that?"

I take a big breath. "Cyn, are you running drugs?"

I wait for her to laugh, or to say I really am crazy, but she just shrugs.

"You are?" My stomach drops. "Jesus, Cyn."

She avoids my eyes. "I know what I'm doing."

I cannot believe she is saying this! "You could end up in jail!"

"Apparently, I'm a cute girl. Apparently, I like to shop. Border guards don't bother with cute girls who like to shop. I go to the mall, make a purchase. If I ever get inspected at the border, I will just say someone made me their fool and planted it on my car when I was in the store. It happens."

I shake my head. "It sounds like you *are* a drug dealer's fool."

She grabs both of my hands. "I didn't tell you because I thought you'd leave me. I'm not a bad person, Daniel."

"You have to stop." I give her hands a tug. "I mean it. No more." When she doesn't reply, I say, "There is nothing that is so bad you can't walk away from it."

She sighs. "I'm not so sure." She takes out her car keys and hands them to me. "Here. You drive. We're going to my house."

Chapter Nine

We exit from the main highway into a subdivision of acreages. The homes are well lit and neatly fenced, with long, winding driveways. These are the kinds of places where people have horses and gardens and sell fresh eggs at the roadway. "Nice neighborhood," I say.

"Keep driving," Cyn says.

We turn onto a driveway barely visible in a bank of trees. The car lurches into a pothole, and the headlights bounce up onto the wall of trees on either side of the road. From up ahead I can hear bass notes thumping, like we're driving to a party. Cyn says, "This is far enough." She unrolls her window. "Turn off the car."

Cyn doesn't make a move to get out. I say, "This is your place? I thought your parents were away."

She gives me a puzzled look.

I say, "Mila said they were in Hawaii."

She holds her hand up as if to shush me. Clearly, her parents are back, because I hear a man's voice and a woman's. I'm not sure if the woman is laughing or crying. A dog barks, and the man's voice lifts into a curse. The dog stops barking. There's a sound of glass breaking, like a bottle. The music stops.

Cyn looks straight ahead. "Wait for it," she says.

There is the sound of someone being slapped—hard. Cyn winces. The woman cries out. Another slap. The man is swearing, using words even Maxwell and I don't use. There's a whining sound from the woman or the dog, I can't tell which.

I move my hand toward the car door. Cyn stops me from opening it. Her eyes are half hooded, and she's shivering. "No," she says. "We need to go."

Another slapping sound, and something crashes onto the floor. I say, "We should call the police, at least."

"The neighbors have probably already called." Her shoulders slump. "Just go."

I start the car and she closes the window. I turn the car around and make our way out to the highway. In the rearview mirror, the light from the house gets smaller and then disappears. Cyn pulls her knees up into her chest. Her hair falls across her face like a curtain. I think about the bruise on her arm.

I say, "You have to leave."

"Exactly."

"You could leave tonight. Stay at my place."

"No. I've got things under control."

"Are you sure, Cyn? You cannot trust some drug dealer to fix your life."

She rubs her temples.

I say, "Just turn him in. The cops will protect you."

"He knows where I live, Daniel."

"So? Let your parents figure it out."

She taps her fingers against her forehead. "He knows where I live because he supplies my mother with heroin. I work for him, he gives my mother what she needs, and my old man doesn't look so bad. And as bad as my old man is, he's better than my mother turning tricks to buy her drugs."

I am having a tough time imagining a soccer mom, possibly with a Hawaiian tan, working the sex trade. But then,

I can't imagine why Cyn's mom would stay with a guy who beats her up. None of it makes sense.

"So you carry stuff across the border for him?"

Cyn nods.

I have to ask. "And that time I went, was I carrying something?"

She hugs her knees. "I couldn't really say."

I slam the dashboard with the heel of my hand. "But you just let me go? What if I'd been pulled out for inspection? I am not exactly a cute girl, Cyn."

Sitting like she is, she looks so small right now. She says, "They wouldn't have pulled you over."

"How do you know that?"

"You weren't afraid," she says, "You didn't know you were taking anything across. You looked normal, like a kid going across for gas. They wouldn't suspect you."

"But you're afraid, so you got me to do it. You sent me to do some scumbag work for some d-bag drug dealer you used to sleep with, and maybe are still sleeping with, because what the hell do I know? What do I know about you at all?" I downshift and floor the gas pedal, burying the tach. "Well, I know this. If you don't have a car, you can't run drugs." I pull into the fast lane and blow past three cars.

Cyn grabs the dash. "Slow down!"

The speedometer reads twenty over.

"I mean it, Daniel. Slow this car down!"

I shift and grind my foot into the gas pedal. Ahead, blue and red lights start to flash.

Cyn starts to cry.

As I go through the speed trap, the speedometer reads forty over. Cops are jumping into their cars, and sirens are blaring. I let the car slow to a crawl and pull over to the side.

Cyn looks at me like I've lost my mind. She says, "You have no idea what you just did."

Chapter Ten

Cyn is a no-show at school the next day, and she ignores my texts. Last night, she was so mad she wouldn't speak to me. The car got impounded for seven days. I have to say, I wasn't expecting the impound fee to be so expensive. But if Dove wants the car, he can pay the fee. Or the car can sit in the impound

lot until it gets sold for non-payment.
I really do not care. And I don't care that
I got a speeding ticket that will take me a
year to pay. Cyn's not driving anywhere
for a while—that's what's important.

After school I'm heading out to the
bus loop when I hear a horn toot and see
Megan pulling up beside me. I jump in
her car.

"Shh," Megan says, motioning to
the backseat. I turn to see Livy asleep in
her car seat. One of her shoes has fallen
off—that kid cannot keep both shoes
on when she's in her car seat. Megan
talks as she drives. "I had my last class
yesterday, so Livy and I had the day
together to celebrate. She wanted to
surprise you and give you a ride home
after school." Megan looks in her rearview mirror. "I must have worn her out
at the playground. She was asleep as
soon as I put her in her seat."

Livy's hair is tousled from being outside, and her cheeks are pink. I say, "I'm glad you guys could hang out."

Megan nods. "I didn't think I'd ever be finished school. I don't know what I'd do without Mom and you."

I must look as surprised as I feel because she says, "I know, I know. I never acknowledge all your help with Livy."

"Well," I say, "the time she puked mac and cheese all down my shirt exceeded the job description. And when she stuck the Smartie up her nose and I had to go after it with tweezers."

"You did that too when you were a little kid. You cried so hard you had chocolate-colored snot running out of your nose. It completely put me off Smarties." Megan glances again in her rearview mirror. "But you won't be on tweezer detail much longer. I got a job. I'm getting my own place."

She's moving out? That means I can take a leak without first moving a kiddie seat off the toilet. I swallow. That means Livy won't be there.

I say, "Where?"

"Well, not here. I'll be working downtown, so I got a suite on the east side."

"Mom works downtown. She commutes from here."

"She spends hours on the bus each day. I can't do that—I'd never see Livy. The place I found is less than half an hour from work, and there's a daycare close by. There's even a little park with a playground."

"It sounds like a done deal."

"I sure hope so." She pats her handbag. "I've saved enough tips from my salon clients for first and last month's rent." She looks at me. "You could sound a bit more excited for me."

"I am, I guess. But isn't the east side kind of rough?"

"I'll lock my door, obviously."

"Obviously. But what about walking to your apartment? What about Livy playing at the park?"

"Shit goes down everywhere, Daniel. It's not like Meridian is some magic kingdom." She rolls her eyes. "Like, no one ever gets shot in Meridian."

My stomach feels like a stone has dropped into it. She's right. I will never, ever take Livy to Meridian Park.

She continues, "Maybe you and Mom should move too."

"You have room for us?"

She laughs—hard. "Yeah. No. It's tiny. Get your own damn place."

I feel tears prickle my eyes, and I take a few deep breaths to stop them. It's always been Mom and Megan and me, and then when Livy was born, it was us four. It's always been just us. Megan must sense how I'm feeling because her voice softens and she says,

"I'll miss you too, Daniel. Livy and I will be fine."

We pull onto our street, and Megan finds a parking spot in front of the building. A car rumbles past and she says, "That is so weird. That thing was behind us the whole way home."

I ratchet my head to see the vehicle. My stomach knots. It's an SUV, an ice-blue Navigator, going slowly. I can't see the driver, but I don't have to. It must be Dove. And he must be pissed.

Megan gets out and reaches into the back to get Livy.

"No, I'll get her," I say. My hands tremble as I undo Livy's seat-belt harness. She barely stirs as I lift her from the car seat. Her head rests on my shoulder. She smells like the playground, of dust and metal and fresh air. I breathe her in, trying to calm myself. Megan bends down to grab the loose shoe from the floor of the car.

The Navigator has turned around and is driving back toward us. I pull Livy close and cover her with my jacket.

The driver guns it, and the SUV thunders past us. The driver turns to give me a long look. He's wearing a hat and dark glasses, but the message seems clear. He knows who I am and he knows where I live. And he knows about Livy. My heart hammers my ribs.

Megan lifts her head. "Who *is* that?"

I try to keep my voice from trembling. "Who knows? Just some idiot. He probably didn't like the way you were driving." With my one free hand I fish out my house keys. My hands are shaking so badly the keys jangle. "Come on, let's get inside."

Indoors, I lay Livy on the couch and tuck a blanket around her. I stand for a minute, watching her sleep. Maybe it is good that Megan and Livy will be moving out—Dove won't know where they've gone.

I go to the window. Below, the street is quiet—people haven't started coming home from work yet. It will be dark when Mom walks home from the bus stop. She'll have her earbuds in, and she'll be thinking about what to make for supper. She won't have any reason to think she might not be safe. I draw the curtains.

But she's not safe. None of us are.

My hands are shaking, but I punch out a message to Cyn. **What did you tell Dove?**

In less than a minute, my phone buzzes. It's Cyn's number on the call display. I pick up.

But it's not Cyn. A man's voice says, "Listen, peckerhead, I don't know who you are, but you better stop texting my girlfriend. She does not want to talk to you. And she sure as shit doesn't want to talk to you about me."

Chapter Eleven

I waited all last night for Cyn to call me so I could break up with her. She never called. Maxwell texted me at the same time he was texting with Mila. So then Mila weighed in and said Cyn must be nuts if she was still with Dove. She said Cyn always liked a bit of excitement. She said when they were younger, Cyn would walk into a store in the mall, pick up some random piece of clothing and walk out. Once she almost got caught but managed to drop what she'd stolen into a garbage can. The stuff Cyn took was never anything she really wanted, Mila said. Cyn just wanted the rush of walking out with it. Mila said Cyn's stunts made them laugh. I know what she's saying. When I'm with Cyn, I feel she gives me this super-charge of confidence. It's like I can do anything. Mila continued, though, and said that when Cyn started with Dove, she changed. It was like all that energy turned inward. She said that what used to draw her to Cyn drove her away.

The next day, at my locker, I feel Cyn's presence before I see her standing there staring at me, her arms crossed. For a quick second I forget that we're not together, but the look on her face freezes me. Quietly, so no one else can hear, she says, "Don't ever text me about Dove."

"I thought he drove by my house, Cyn. My house!" I pause. "That is, until I found out he was with you."

She pulls me into an empty class-room and closes the door. "Someone drove by your house?"

"A big Navigator SUV."

"What color was it?"

"Kind of a light blue."

"Oh." She looks at the floor. Her runners, the ones she bought when we were together, are muddy, like she walked across the park. One of her socks has slipped down into the runner.

She is so still it's like she's forgotten I'm there. I nudge her. "Cyn?"

She looks at me. Her eyes are wet. "I know that Navigator. It's someone Dove works for."

"You mean, someone your boyfriend works for."

"He's not my boyfriend."

"He certainly thinks he is. And you're acting like he is."

"I'm not going to lie. It is getting complicated."

I can't help but laugh. "You not lying—that would be a nice change."

"Daniel, I am so scared. I'm scared you're going to leave me, and I really, really need you not to leave me right now."

I am trying hard not to lose it with her. "I know things at your house are pretty messed up. But what you're doing is serious, Cyn. And you've got me pulled into it too. Your boyfriend's buddy is driving by my house—"

She interrupts. "He's not my boyfriend. And the guy who drove by your house isn't a buddy. Not at all. He's putting pressure on Dove."

I think about the shootings that have happened lately. My head starts to throb.

She continues, "You don't have anything to rip off, and you don't mean anything to Dove. He was probably just trying to scare you."

"Well, he did. How does he know about me?"

She shakes her head. "Someone saw us together maybe."

She really does seem scared. I say, "The Navigator. Has it been by your house too?"

Her shoulders slump. "I'm alone in the house, and we have a security system, but I'm still afraid that he's going to break in. Normal people keep their lights on and make it look like there is someone in the house. Me, I keep it dark and let the newspapers pile up on the porch."

"What about your parents?"

She sighs. "They're in Hawaii. They're not back for a couple of weeks."

"So they *are* away. With Mila's parents, right?"

She looks puzzled, like she can't remember what she's told me. "Yes."

"But you took me to your house. All hell was breaking loose. Your dad was yelling. Your mom was crying."

Cyn stays quiet.

I feel the hair on my arms lift into goose bumps. "But that wasn't your parents," I say. I make myself take a deep breath. "You don't live in that house."

She shakes her head. "No. They are our neighbors. We hear them fighting. It's like clockwork—the guy gets home, they start drinking, they fight."

Watching Cyn is like watching a magician reveal her tricks. "And your mother doesn't use drugs."

I can barely hear her answer. "No."

Layer by layer, it becomes clear. There was no magic to her deception—

if I'd had my eyes open, I would have seen her sleight of hand. But, just like a magician, she relied on my believing in her. "You wouldn't take me to your real house. You wouldn't let me into your real world. Because then nothing would make sense. Like that you sleep with a drug dealer. And that he bought you a car so you could run drugs for him across the border. I guess your parents are okay with all that."

She throws up her arms, exasperated. "They don't know about Dove. My parents think Dove is my boss at the restaurant and that I work late sometimes. He didn't buy me the car. They did." Her voice starts to shake. "They said they would rather I drive my own car than ride in a guy's."

I blink. "In the time we've been together, have you told me *anything* that's true?"

She takes my hands and holds them against her chest. "Don't ask for the truth and then make me sound like I'm some kind of villain."

"No one ever thinks they are the villain."

"I am not a bad person, Daniel."

"I don't think you are. I just don't understand why you do it. It doesn't seem like your family is short on money." I study her face. What would make her take such crazy risks? I hate to ask it, but I have to. "Cyn, do you love this guy?"

"No." She looks me in the eye. "Maybe I did in the beginning, but I was an idiot." She drops her head. "He used me. Right from the start, he knew what he wanted me for. So I did a run, and he made me do another. And when I said I didn't want to do any more, he said I had to or he'd get killed. He gets so angry." She folds her arms across herself. "And rough."

I think of the marks on Cyn's arm. Whatever else she has said, those marks were real. My hands clench into fists.

She says, "And I could tolerate his rage." She starts to cry. "But he showed me a picture once that he took of me. I was asleep on his bed. It's the kind of picture a girl does not want shared." She glances at me. "I'm sorry, but you may as well know."

I feel my face redden. "That you weren't exactly a virgin? I guess I knew. I mean, I didn't really have much to go on, because you were my first."

She touches my arm. "You are such a good guy." She sighs. "I begged him to delete the photo, but he said it's harmless, that it's just for him. But he showed the picture to me. It's like he wanted me to know he has it. Even if he doesn't post it, he'll make sure my parents know who I am."

"So you're not perfect. You screwed up. Your parents will get over it. Go to the cops, Cyn."

"No." She looks terrified. "Don't even talk like that. That would get us all killed."

I try to say something, but she holds up her hands. "No," she says, "you have to understand. The cross-border thing? Money goes one way. Other stuff comes back across."

My mouth feels suddenly dry. "Stuff? Like what kind of stuff?"

"Like drugs. Weapons."

My throat sticks, and I can't talk.

She says, "So now Dove has obligations he can't keep." She puts her hands on top of mine. I try to pull my hands away, but she grips them hard.

"I begged Dove to stop sending me," she says. "Even he knows that I've lost my nerve. The other night was going to be my last run. I was supposed to be done with him. But then the car got impounded."

I find my voice. "By me. I got the car impounded."

She says, "I have to do one more run. That's it."

"You can just pay him. Ask your parents for the money."

"It would kill them to know what I've been doing."

I think about my sister's money she has saved for rent. I'll have to steal it, and then my sister won't be able to move, and she might lose out on the job. "I can get some cash."

Cyn shakes her head. "It won't be enough."

"But how can you do a run? Your car is impounded."

"I can get another car."

Of course she can. Her parents probably have another car in the garage. Maybe they have two or three. I was stupid to think I could fix the problem by getting the car impounded.

"You'll get caught, Cyn. Dove is right. You're too scared—it's all over your face. The border guards will know that something isn't right."

"I'm less scared to get caught by the border guards. With them, I have a chance." She goes to put her arms around me, but I don't let her.

I say, "You used me just like Dove used you."

She nods. "I did."

"Gee, thanks, Cyn. Now you decide not to lie."

"I'm sorry." Her eyes fill. "But part of me is glad. I mean, I am sorry you're in this mess. But I don't regret for a minute being with you. The way you treated me, I started to believe I was good. I want to be a good person, Daniel. You have to believe me—I want to be with you."

"I'd like to believe you. But being his girlfriend or being mine won't change who you are." I turn to walk out the door. "You know, when we kissed, you never closed your eyes."

She says, "If you know that, then you didn't either."

Chapter Twelve

The night of the dance is clear and cold.
Outside the school, people line two
sides of a table where school liaison
cops are searching bags for liquor and
drugs. Most of the girls aren't wearing
coats over their dresses, and they huddle
in the line, rubbing their arms against
the cold. The cop who spoke to me in
the hallway is there, Constable Nagle.

He sees me and his gaze holds mine for a second. I jam my hands in my pockets. My new jacket isn't warm enough—I'm freezing too.

"Hey, nice jacket." Maxwell comes up behind me and gives me a shove.

I shove him back. "Is that hairspray I smell?" I say.

He pats his hair. "I love that it's not raining. Wearing a hood just flattens it." Maxwell looks around. "Am I right in guessing you aren't standing out here waiting for me?"

"If you're asking if I'm waiting for Cyn, then no, I'm not. I haven't even seen her in days."

"So you're just waiting outside because you like standing around freezing?"

I can't help but look in the direction of the parking lot. I can't help but hope that she'll show. If she walked out of the darkness right now, just walked up to me and said she's done with Dove, and we went on to live the most boring existence on earth, then I'd be happy.

Mila runs over from the line and encircles Maxwell's waist with her arms. She's wearing a little strapless dress I know my sister would love. She's carrying a single red rose. Her hair is loose except for two tiny braids on each side. It looks good that way. Maxwell wraps her in his jacket. I'm sure my eyebrows shoot up, because Maxwell grins over her shoulder at me. "People win the lottery," he says.

I say, "You guys should go in. I'll find you in there."

"No way." He turns to Mila. "We're going to Meridian Park. Mr. Responsible here wants to see if Cyn is coming to the dance."

I am mortified that he can read me so well. I say, "Cyn won't be there. And even if she is, it's not like we're together."

Mila falls into step between Maxwell and me. "You should be. She really likes you."

We use our phones to light the way across the field. The frozen grass crunches under our feet. Mila is tiptoeing in her heels, so Maxwell swings her up onto his back. She squeals, "I'm going to fall out of my dress!"

We make it to the bench, empty in its pool of light. Cyn isn't there, of course. I knew she wouldn't be. She made her choice. Still, my voice shakes when I say, "She's not coming. Let's just go back to the school."

Then Mila says, "Wait, that's her!"

I turn to see a gray sedan pulling into the lot.

"Where?" I say.

Mila points to the gray car. "That's her mom's car."

It is Cyn. She gets out of the car. She's wearing a dress with a sparkly top and a short, full skirt. Her hair is loose and swings around her shoulders. Cyn sees me in the light of the bench, and her face breaks into a smile. She waves.

"She looks amazing," Mila sighs.

She does. She looks like nothing is wrong. I can see she's wearing her new heels. Maxwell, Mila and I move out of the light and start walking toward her.

Another vehicle is driving into the parking lot. It is an ice-blue Navigator SUV. Cyn looks over her shoulder and then to us. Fear traces her face.

"No." I blink, hoping I'm imagining it. But the SUV veers straight toward Cyn. Shots pop.

Maxwell says, "What the…?"

Cyn has started to run. The Navigator's engine revs, and its tires spin. I hear footsteps running up behind me, and my heart jumps into my throat. Someone shoulders me onto the ground. It's the cop. "Stay down!" he growls.

I have to get to Cyn. There's more gunfire, and I can't find my footing on the frozen ground. I feel the cop grab at my legs. Cyn is running, her eyes wide. I think she's calling something, but the cop is yelling into his radio and I can't hear. The SUV is skidding sideways. I see the back window is open and the flash as the gun fires.

I kick myself free and scramble to my feet. The cop curses. I start to run. "Cyn!"

Another shot, and she's hit. She spirals with the impact. She turns toward me, holding her shoulder. I know she's looking for me. I flash my phone. A bullet explodes in the ground beside me, and dirt peppers my face. I can hear the cop screaming at me. "GET DOWN!" I hear gunfire behind me, and a window on the SUV shatters.

I'm close enough now to see that Cyn is crying. She's clutching her shoulder, running. Somewhere, sirens howl. The SUV spins. A gun fires. Cyn lifts off the ground, her hair a dark sunburst around her head. Her eyes seem to find mine as she falls.

The SUV peels out of the parking lot into a sea of red and blue flashing lights. Maybe the tires on the SUV blow, I don't know. It rolls onto its side, a comet of sparks arcing off the pavement. I'm on my knees beside Cyn. I'm cradling her face in my hands, and I'm calling her name, again and again. Her eyes are closed, and I'm begging her to open them, to look at me, to say she's okay.

But she doesn't.

The cop falls to his knees beside me. Sweat beads his forehead. He immediately checks Cyn's neck for a pulse. I watch him, willing him to feel something. It takes so long. His hands are shaking. He positions his hands to do CPR. Blood darkens his hands, his sleeves.

He does one compression and then stops.
His hands have fallen into Cyn's chest.
It's like her heart has been blown away.

"Try. Please try," I say.

But he just kneels there, his hands
trembling.

Cyn's blood is a river under my knees.
Someone sets a shoe down beside Cyn,
the strap broken and crystals strewn.
Paramedics arrive and pull the cop
aside. Someone says I have to move, so
I do. A camera flashes again and again
on her fallen form.

Did she do the last run? Did she
refuse? Was killing her some kind of
message to Dove?

I feel Maxwell beside me. I say, "She
couldn't run in those shoes. She couldn't
get away." My voice shudders. "She got
caught in the crossfire, that's all."

Maxwell looks like he's deciding
whether to believe Cyn is really an

innocent bystander. Even to me, my words sound hollow. He says, "This much I know, my friend. She was dressed to go dancing."

Chapter Thirteen

Livy hands me a stack of books and climbs up onto my knee. Her hair, still damp from her bath, curls around her face. At the edge of the room next to the heat vents, her snowsuit, hat and mittens are laid out to dry. Outside our window, the streetlight catches the snow, falling like silver feathers. Snow is piled along the street where plows have pushed it into mountains. Livy sighs happily as she settles into my lap.

Megan's apartment is small, like ours. Our old place was bigger, but Mom is happy to live closer to work. Maxwell and Mila crash on the couch when they visit. Livy loves her new daycare. Megan likes her job.

Mom and Megan thought we had to move. When I told Mom and Megan about what had been going on, they freaked, of course. They thought I'd be a target. I don't think so. I only know what Cyn told me, and she didn't tell me much. I don't know enough even to testify.

Someone is testifying though. In the news, the informant is referred to as Person X. All I know is that Dove's restaurant is closed and he's vanished. Whether Person X identifies Cyn as the target, I don't know. Maybe being his girl-friend was her only crime. Maybe Cyn's parents can hang on to their daughter as they knew her. Maybe I can too.

Sometimes, when I dream, Cyn is laughing at something. Her hair is loose like it was that night, like a dark sea on her shoulders. She never looks at me in my dream, but I wake up glad that she looked happy.

Livy pats my cheek. "Uncle Daniel, read!" She puts a book into my hands.

I look at the book. "Livy, we've read this one about nineteen times."

She jabs her finger at the cover. "Cinderella is my favorite."

Livy has stopped asking about Cyn. I told her that Cyn moved away too, and that's why we wouldn't see her again. She accepted my story, and why wouldn't she? Or maybe she knew I was lying and let me have the fantasy. Either way, she believes in me, and I take a lot of strength from that.

I open the book to the first page. "Okay, but I just have to say, the princess should have worn shoes that stayed on her feet."

"Shhh," she says. "Don't tell me what happens."

Acknowledgments

I am grateful for the leg up from Shelley Hrdlitschka and Kim Denman, the best writing group ever, and to Andrew and the Orca team.

Diane Tullson has written a number of novels about difficult topics, including *Lockdown* and *Riley Park*. She lives in Delta, British Columbia. For more information, visit www.dianetullson.com.

orca soundings

For more information on all the books
in the Orca Soundings series, please visit
www.orcabook.com.